PETAGONIA PETS

GROSSET & DUNLAP
Published by the Penguin Group
Penguin Group (USA) Inc., 375 Hudson Street, New York, New York 10014, USA
Penguin Group (Canada), 90 Eglinton Avenue East, Suite 700,
Toronto, Ontario M4P 2Y3, Canada
(a division of Pearson Penguin Canada Inc.)
Penguin Books Ltd., 80 Strand, London WC2R 0RL, England
Penguin Group Ireland, 25 St. Stephen's Green, Dublin 2, Ireland
(a division of Penguin Books Ltd.)
Penguin Group (Australia), 250 Camberwell Road, Camberwell, Victoria 3124, Australia
(a division of Pearson Australia Group Pty. Ltd.)
Penguin Books India Pvt. Ltd., 11 Community Centre, Panchsheel Park,
New Delhi—110 017, India
Penguin Group (NZ), 67 Apollo Drive, Rosedale, Auckland 0632, New Zealand
(a division of Pearson New Zealand Ltd.)
Penguin Books (South Africa) (Pty.) Ltd., 24 Sturdee Avenue,
Rosebank, Johannesburg 2196, South Africa

Penguin Books Ltd., Registered Offices: 80 Strand, London WC2R 0RL, England

Published by Grosset & Dunlap, a division of Penguin Young Readers Group, 345 Hudson Street,
New York, New York 10014. GROSSET & DUNLAP is a trademark of Penguin Group (USA) Inc.
Printed in the U.S.A.

ISBN 978-0-448-45785-7   10 9 8 7 6 5 4 3 2 1

PETAGONIA PETS

by Lana Edelman
illustrated by Artful Doodlers

Grosset & Dunlap
An Imprint of Penguin Group (USA) Inc.

Welcome to Petagonia,

the Zoobles land of pets!

Petagonia is a beautiful place,

full of trees and flowers.

It also has a river where Zoobles can splish and splash together. Catlin, Doxy, and Ears are Zoobles who live in Petagonia.

Catlin is an adventurous cat.

She always has a smile

on her face.

Doxy is a playful dog.

He has a lot of energy.

Ears is a funny bunny.

He likes to make

his friends laugh.

Look!

A pink ball rolls down the tree.

It is going so fast!

But it is not just a pink ball.

That ball is Catlin!

Catlin bounces

onto her Happitat.

Pop!

She can see all of Petagonia

from the top of her Happitat!

Catlin sings with the blue birds.

The birds fly above her

as they sing.

Can you sing along?

Look!

Here comes Doxy the Dog.

Doxy is a very active Zooble.

He likes to roll around Petagonia,
kick a ball, and play in the sun.

Doxy waters a tree

to make flowers grow.

The flowers are bright pink
and very pretty.

They smell nice, too!

Hop! Hop! Hop!

Look!

Here comes Ears the Bunny.

Ears hops very high.

How high do you think

he can hop?

Ears does tricks to make

Doxy and Catlin laugh.

He hops onto the stone bridge,

flips, splashes in the river,

and then hops back

onto the grass.

Catlin, Doxy, and Ears

love to play games together.

They hop after one another

on the grass and

the stone bridge.

Their favorite game

is the Bounce & Trounce.

Catlin, Doxy, and Ears race

down the hill as balls.

Then they zoom through the air!

They grab flowers, stars,

and berries as they go.

At the bottom of the hill,
Catlin, Doxy, and Ears
bounce onto their Happitats.

They pop open.

That was so much fun!

At night, Catlin, Doxy, and Ears practice jumping onto their Happitats and popping open. Who can pop open the fastest?

Then Catlin hides

behind her Happitat.

Will Doxy and Ears find her?

It has been a long day.

Catlin, Doxy, and Ears have

played so many games!

But now they are tired.

It is time to go to sleep.

Catlin, Doxy, and Ears

roll up in their Happitats.

Good night, Zoobles, sleep tight.

There will be more games

to play tomorrow!

Zoobles!
SPRING TO LIFE!™

PETAGONIA PETS

EAN

ISBN 978-0-448-45785-7

9 780448 457857

5 0 3 9 9 >